*Table of Co*ntents

Part I: Creation:

- The Beginning of Us

Part II: Chaos, Connectivity & the Great Divide:

- The End of Us

Part III: Actualizations

- A Glimpse:

Epilogue:

- What Follows in Eternity

Part I: Creation

…Few and small, these memories escape me…I remember to dream, and to awake from sleep…

The Beginning of Us

In the beginning, there was an idea of *Us*. That idea became the reality of *Us*, an energy, a form, a purpose. It started off small, unimaginably and perceptually small, but *Our* purpose made *Us* grow.

We did not know each other yet, for *We* were inseparable, two forms in synchronicity unaware of *Our* purpose joined from the beginning of eternity. From void to darkness to fire and light, *We* traveled together.

As *We* grew, so too did *Our* direction to be more than what *We* were. Time, being relative, can still feel like an eternity when seen within the reflections of one's own circumstance.

We traveled millions of years through dense fire. Always together—I can feel that now—but all that was taken for granted in the moment. And though *We* were of the fire, molded by it, *We* were more. *We* were an idea realized and formed into being, destined to be more than what *We* were or are now.

An awareness of transition, space and time became cold and vast. Together *We* raced across the darkness, unique and bright as millions of others hidden from the sight I have now. And as *We* raced farther from where *We* began, *We* began to change.

This change made *Us* learn to want to identify *Us* as parts. Those parts of us wanted to stay together with the knowledge of *Us*. But we could not, for we were always two parts of the same idea and it was time to be so—it was time for us to play our individual parts. Even the vastness of space began to slow down, thicken, and coalesce around us.

Our bond was strong and we would not be parted so easily. We became complementary, no longer *Oneself* or *Ourselves*, but parts of a whole in our refusal to separate completely. This made us want to be together always, yet the instinct to be alone and by ourselves had been born—this gave each of us new weight.

Then fire separated the skies in two, blue beneath and the perpetual lighted darkness above. This fire burned and repelled as we were pulled into the blue. Weight tore us apart as we hit ground and our beings became elemental. Dissolving and coalescing infinitely until we could not hold onto each other in ways more than just memory. It was a feeling never felt before, something visceral, a pain actualized for the first time—that first moment of emotional cognizance and loss.

Apart, we gravitated towards the things we were made from the most, and the elements which we were similar to. We became whole and flesh; but we would always be incomplete. Our purpose was not to be held alone—that purpose that was once and always will be an idea formed into reality, that idea of *Us*.

She became *feminine,* the fire upon the wind, and I *masculine*, the stone in the sea. Time dissolved into tasks. Endless aging and death, rebirth and discovery. Each death brought us closer to individual thought and awareness beyond just connectivity of our environments; until at last we became individuals. Individuals torn and unique, bound to our properties and always in search for what was lacking in ourselves.

In body we were whole, but in spirit we were incomplete. That energy, that purpose which once coursed through *Us* from the moment of *Our* conception had parted. It made the world polarized against us; and nothing, no matter how comforting, could sustain our peace alone.

She would always long for oceans and the seas, the calm, cool depths to surround her and ease the fire in her heart; as I would need the pulse of fire to warm my heart into action; its beauty to whisper in my ear like the wind and compel the granite of my heart towards compassion.

The measure of time, though, made us who we are now, and cannot be ignored. Countless ages full of new meaning and experiences beyond what was once just *Us* has taken hold as strong as any single bond. *We* became separate and found new meaning and identity alone, sacred as any unified purity, for it is all we know of ourselves now.

In this identity, we would still long for the comforts in what we now knew as current truths for so long in time and cognizance. We would long for whatever we weren't but always needed what made us who we are. It pulls us apart as much as it draws us together. Fire, light, breath, and the weighted darkness of the deep will always be at the center of who we've become.

Together in time, we will eternally chase each other, being so much more than whom we have become when reunited…and longing when we are apart…

I will never be whole without you; we are more than just external means; we are eternal measures of joy and love.

I will love you always

*

Part II:

Chaos, Connectivity

&

the Great Divide

...As I remember and live these words, I am reminded of other truths along the way. This eternal chase set out for me will not be equal for all.

No matter where or how we came to be, all things all futures are forced by the measures of who we have become. Our choices, our births, our individual pains allow for corruption. We become as clear and transparent as if we were made of glass; given that each eternal pair will become individualized and unique, and form their own eternal loop.

Some may suffer more than others; some may feel no longing or loss from time or time apart. For some, the memory alone will suffice.

I can only note the fate for what is mine and speculate on the fates of others...

The End of Us

    I will not reach whatever end is to be in this life with the one I love. *We all transition alone; we all die alone—no matter one's belief.*

    What we experience in the afterlife, that moment of transition will be our own.
I would be a moment shared only by those who have gone before and leaving all those living behind.

    That moment where we do not understand, yet others cannot follow.   I will grieve or be grieved at that moment.

    I am left with hope and empirical thoughts. I am left to grieve and wonder in every moment; in every moment wasted now by self-indulgences that hurt no one but myself—those brief joyous deaths.

True love reveals itself like a painting, not a sculpture. Sculptures, statues, and carvings are stripped of what they are to become and what the world wants of them. Whereas romance, compassion and love are ideas and concepts added to a surface once void of depth, until it becomes perfect.

Death will not feel like a sculpture. Death will be like a photograph, something taken not drawn, like pieces of us that are forever wrong. No matter how beautiful the design or its image, it will be a loss. It is a still frame that took no time to build, but shows everything in the grace it once had. It's a reminder without substance or injuries out of context, like painted scars only for presentation.

But how will death come?

It is the nature of fire to consume and burn out quickly and leave its mark; to cleanse, punish, or inspire all around it, but, also to flash for a brief moment.

Fire that lives to burn as a cinder is a slow death. They suffer a lie in life, devoid of passion. It is a fate they rarely suffer, and one fire rarely wishes to endure; and it is one we would never forget if witnessed.

We remember the fire in life. We remember those whose eyes burned so brightly against the darkness and confusion of this world. If their eyes turn pale, it's a sadness we cannot endure, and for them to extinguish is a pain we cannot ignore…

But water and stone drown;

taking the heat, the wind, and the fire. No matter how it is formed or shaped, stone endures. No matter if it's beneath the seas or molten, earth remains until fire completely consumes it.

But it is not a glorious fate to be the pebble at the bottom of the ocean floor or as random as any drop of rain within the clouds. It is their fate to either have the will of fire broken upon their backs or to completely put out the fire that so inspires…

At times it may seem the wisest thing to do; to stymie the rage and destruction of fire. But that course of action is still without question a death.

If fire is joined with earth or water, then, it will die slowly and sadly, but die non-the-less.

Fire and air, earth and water, they can make mountains though. Death and life in a recurrent cycle, elevating life out of molten seas and chaos to live in the sun for all the world to see. Fire and ice can come from the sky as it can from the sea.

I am water and earth. She is fire and air. She inspires me, moves me. I temper her rage and feel her wrath.

We love completely, which is why I lament all the little things leading up to this moment.

I would hold onto her like a drowning man. In her arms, I would die if I could be so selfish—but I would lose in that moment.

It makes every thought, every gesture, every loving, passionate intent a hypocritical lie because I am not holding onto her. I am destroying her by my nature.

But then she comes to me…

She mends my broken wings and instead of burning me with chastisement, harsh words on barbed tongues, she gives me wings and wind for flight.

In those moments, those present moments, I am happy. I can only pray that we are eternally happy in this slow death…

With her death, my life would become void of love where only memories would remain, without the substance and beauty of being in the present moment with her.

I would be like a pulverized stone at the bottom of the ocean, small and insignificant as a piece of sand in the dark of the deep, waiting for its eternity to begin.

I would be waiting for the hell of this karma to end…

But she has it in herself to turn me into dust, bellowing in a swirl of wind as countless and peculiar as any grain of sand that lines the ocean floor. To push the life in me, to burn it out. To end me so completely that whatever I could have called myself would be gone.

She will be void of her stability, her earth her stone. She will be void of her calm, her water carried away like steam.

What becomes of the fire that exhausted itself? Alone and paled to cinder without its crux that challenged and soothed, that took its fury? What life remains?

We are the fates of one another, repeating, eternal. I've seen both endings, both transitions—*and at present*, death has stirred in me. Death has given me a glimpse of what could come when my candle is spent, when the fire in me is finally

extinguished…

Part III:

Actualizations:

...Here comes heaven again; a perfect and complete thought of her; then a moment...Transition...

A Glimpse

In transition of thought, I become lost in space and time… I become a possibility.

A glimpse of understanding in that transition; to articulate a hope and the words experienced…

I am chasing her again, like a pull from an anchor. Life ebbs away as I am propelled forward. I am cold, separate but satisfied. I am dizzy and almost drunk in how fast I seem to move compared to everything around me…Sound calls me. A distant echo pulling me towards what I know to be home.

I am traversing the darkness and space towards a light that draws me in like gravity. It has no shape, but I know it. I am completed by it, within it, with it. I am whole again without time, relevance, or thought…

It was as if a curtain of night was lifted. Like walking into sunlight from behind a deep shadow long embraced. I was in the void, becoming…being…

*

It was a strange sense of reality when my mind bore commonplace emotions again; emotions that were taken for granted until they were perverted or enlightened.

I came back with an understanding of *Us*, more profound than I had before.

Our beliefs actualized in the mind's eye—concepts of heaven or hell—Its ambivalence, complete and unfettered purpose that cannot be shattered by time or creed.

I knew we will lack the senses or tongues to describe it; that moment where we did and would exist together. That chance for understanding, that chance to be all things whole; to be *Us* entirely as that one thought, that one idea.

The End

Epilogue:

What Follows in Eternity

What follows is silent, still,

Full of the music of your laughter;

A gentle voice that breaks the void,

Where I am no longer alone.

"A soulmate is an ongoing connection with another individual that the soul picks up again in various times and places over lifetimes. We are attracted to another person at a soul level not because that person is our unique complement, but because by being with that individual, we are somehow provided with an impetus to become whole ourselves." (Edgar Cayce.)

**

Printed in Great Britain
by Amazon